A WRINKLE IN TIME

Madeleine L'Engle

*sparknotes

*spark notes

SPARKNOTES is a registered trademark of SparkNotes LLC

© 2018 Sterling Publishing Co., Inc.
Cover © 2018 Sterling Publishing, Co., Inc.

ISBN 978-1-4114-7912-8

Distributed in Canada by Sterling Publishing Co., Inc.
c/o Canadian Manda Group, 664 Annette Street
Toronto, Ontario, M6S 2C8, Canada
Distributed in the United Kingdom by GMC Distribution Services
Castle Place, 166 High Street, Lewes, East Sussex, BN7 1XU, England
Distributed in Australia by NewSouth Books
45 Beach Street, Coogee, NSW 2034, Australia

For information about custom editions, special sales, and premium
and corporate purchases, please contact Sterling Special Sales at
800-805-5489 or specialsales@sterlingpublishing.com.

Manufactured in Canada

Lot #:
2 4 6 8 10 9 7 5 3 1

01/18

sterlingpublishing.com
sparknotes.com

Please submit all comments and questions or report errors to sparknotes.com/errors

CONTENTS

CONTEXT

Madeleine L'Engle was born in New York City in 1918 to a foreign correspondent and a gifted pianist. An only child, she had a great love of reading and drawing. After attending several boarding schools in Europe and the United States, L'Engle graduated from Smith College in 1941 and went on to pursue a career in theater. In 1946, she married Hugh Franklin and the couple moved to New York City. There, L'Engle spent her time helping her husband in their general store, raising three children, and writing her first novel.

Today, Madeleine L'Engle has more than 35 books to her name, including science fiction, suspense novels, novels for young adults, poetry, plays, and nonfiction. Nearly all of her books reflect her struggles with Christian theology and her fervent belief in the values of family love and moral responsibility. *A Wrinkle in Time,* one of her earlier novels, is a blend of science fiction and fantasy, aimed at a young-adult audience.

L'Engle has stated that any theory of writing must also be a theory of cosmology: "One cannot discuss structure in writing without discussing structure in all life; it is impossible to talk about why anybody writes a book or paints a picture or composes a symphony without talking about the nature of the universe."*A Wrinkle in Time* reflects a cosmology heavily influenced by Christian theology and modern physics. L'Engle wrote the book as part of her rebellion against Christian piety and her quest for a personal theology. At the time, she was also reading with great interest the new physics of Albert Einstein and Max Planck. L'Engle's ideas about human life and nonlinear time play an important role in this novel and distinguish it from other spiritual and time-travel narratives.

L'Engle initially had tremendous difficulty publishing this novel because publishers could not identify a market for it among either children or adults. L'Engle insisted that she wrote for *people,* because "people read books." For two years, she received rejection after rejection, a frustrating process she describes at length in her autobiography *A Circle of Quiet* (1972). Finally, in 1962, John Farrar of Farrar, Strauss, & Giroux agreed to publish the book even though he did not expect it to sell. To the surprise of the publishing world, the book was wildly successful. It was awarded the 1963 Newberry Medal and has now been translated into more than 15 languages. L'Engle later wrote a whole series about the Murry family called the Time Fantasy series, including *A Wind in the Door* (1973), *A Swiftly Tilting Planet* (1978), *Many Waters* (1986), and *An Acceptable Time* (1996).

PLOT OVERVIEW

A Wrinkle in Time is the story of Meg Murry, a high school–age girl who is transported on an adventure through time and space with her younger brother Charles Wallace and her friend Calvin O'Keefe to rescue her father, a gifted scientist, from the evil forces that hold him prisoner on another planet. At the beginning of the book, Meg is a homely, awkward, but loving, girl, troubled by personal insecurities and her concern for her father, who has been missing for more than a year. The plot begins with the arrival of Mrs. Whatsit at the Murry house on a dark and stormy evening. Although she looks like an eccentric tramp, she is actually a celestial creature with the ability to read Meg's thoughts. She startles Meg's mother by reassuring her of the existence of a tesseract—a sort of "wrinkle" in space and time. It is through this wrinkle that Meg and her companions will travel through the fifth dimension in search of Mr. Murry.

On the afternoon following Mrs. Whatsit's visit, Meg and Charles Wallace walk over to Mrs. Whatsit's cabin. On the way, they meet Calvin O'Keefe, a popular boy in Meg's school whom Charles considers a kindred spirit. The three children learn from Mrs. Whatsit and her friends Mrs. Who and Mrs. Which that the universe is threatened by a great evil called the Black Thing that is taking the form of a giant cloud and engulfing the stars and planets around it. Several planets have already succumbed to this evil force, including Camazotz, the planet on which Mr. Murry is imprisoned.

The three Mrs. W's transport the children to Camazotz and instruct them to remain always in each other's company while on their quest for Mr. Murry. On Camazotz, all objects and places appear exactly alike because the whole planet must conform to the terrifying rhythmic pulsation of IT, a giant disembodied brain. Charles Wallace tries to fight IT with his exceptional intelligence but is overpowered by the evil and becomes a robot-like creature mouthing the words with which IT infuses him. Under the control of IT, Charles leads Meg and Calvin to Mr. Murry and together they confront IT. However, they, too, are unable to withstand IT's power; they escape only at the last minute, when Mr. Murry seizes Meg and Calvin, "tessering" away with them (traveling via another tesseract) to a gray planet called Ixchel inhabited by tall, furry beasts who care for the travelers. Charles Wallace remains possessed by IT, a prisoner of Camazotz.

On planet Ixchel the three Mrs. W's appear once again, and Meg realizes that she must travel alone back to Camazotz to rescue her brother. Mrs. Which tells her that she has one thing that IT does not have, and this will be her weapon against the evil. However, Meg must discover this weapon for herself. When standing in the presence of IT, Meg realizes what this is: her ability to love. Thus, by concentrating on her love for Charles Wallace, she is able to restore him to his true identity. Meg releases Charles from IT's clutches and tessers with him through time and space, landing in her twin brothers' vegetable garden.

CHARACTER LIST

Meg Murry The book's heroine and protagonist—a homely, awkward, but loving high school student—is sent on an adventure through time and space with her brother and her friend Calvin to rescue her father from the evil force that is attempting to take over the universe. Meg's greatest faults are her anger, impatience, and lack of self-confidence, but she channels and overcomes them, ultimately emerging victorious.

Charles Wallace Murry Meg's extraordinarily intelligent five-year-old younger brother who is capable of reading minds and understanding other creatures in a way that none of the other Murry children can.

Calvin O'Keefe A popular boy and talented athlete in Meg's high school who accompanies the Murry children on their adventure. Calvin comes from a large family that does not really care about him, but he nonetheless demonstrates a strong capacity for love and affection, and shows a burgeoning romantic interest in Meg.

IT The disembodied brain that controls all the inhabitants of Camazotz with its revolting, pulsing rhythm. IT, identified with the Black Thing, is the embodiment of evil on this planet.

The Black Thing A cold and dark shadow that symbolizes the evil forces that Meg, Calvin, and Charles Wallace must fight against in order to rescue Mr. Murry.

Mrs. Whatsit The youngest of the three celestial beings who accompany the children on their adventure. Meg initially comes to know Mrs. Whatsit as the tramp who stole bedsheets from their neighbors and then sought shelter from a storm in the Murrys' warm kitchen. She later learns that Mrs. Whatsit gave up her existence as a star in order to fight the Black Thing.

Mrs. Which   The oldest of the three celestial beings who accompany the children on their adventure. Mrs. Which has difficulty materializing and is usually just a shimmering gleam. Her unconventional speech is usually rendered in capitalized words, with the first consonants repeated several times.

Mrs. Who   The second of the three celestial beings who accompany the children on their adventure. She usually speaks in quotations from famous thinkers and writers because she finds it too difficult to craft her own sentences. When the children first meet Mrs. Who, she is sewing sheets in the haunted house in their neighborhood.

Mr. Murry   Meg's father and a physicist who works for a top-secret government agency on experiments with travel through the space-time continuum in the fifth dimension. In trying to tesser to Mars (i.e., travel through a tesseract, or wrinkle in time), he is captured and imprisoned on the dark planet of Camazotz. When the plot begins, no one on Earth has heard from him for more than a year.

Aunt Beast   This tall, furry, many-tentacled inhabitant of the planet Ixchel cares lovingly for Meg after she is nearly destroyed by the Black Thing. Aunt Beast, like all the creatures on Ixchel, lacks eyes and has no concept of light or vision.

The Happy Medium   A jolly, clairvoyant woman in a silk turban and satin gown who shows the children a vision of Earth through her crystal ball. The Happy Medium is reluctant to show them anything unpleasant, but the Mrs. W's insist that they see what they are up against.

Man with the Red Eyes   A robot-like inhabitant of Camazotz who tries to hypnotize Meg, Charles Wallace, and Calvin in the CENTRAL Central Intelligence building. The Man, like all of Camazotz, is totally controlled by the power of IT.

Mrs. Murry Meg's mother and an experimental biologist who works out of a lab in the Murry home. She is at once a brilliant scientist and a loving mother who cooks meals for her family on her Bunsen burner. She also writes loving letters to her absent husband every night.

Mr. Jenkins Meg's cold and unfeeling high-school principal who calls her "belligerent and uncooperative" and implies that her family is in denial about Mr. Murry's true whereabouts.

Mrs. Buncombe The wife of the constable in Meg's hometown, who has twelve bedsheets stolen from her at the beginning of the novel.

Sandy and Dennys Murry Meg's athletic and socially successful ten-year-old twin brothers who encourage her to let them fight off the bullies who make fun of Charles Wallace. The twins do not accompany Meg and Charles Wallace on their interplanetary adventure.

OVERALL ANALYSIS
AND THEMES

A *Wrinkle in Time* is a book about the battle between good and evil and the ultimate triumph of love. Every character is clearly identified with either good or evil: the "good" characters include Meg, her family, Calvin, the Mrs. W's, Aunt Beast, and the Happy Medium. The "evil" characters include IT, The Black Thing, and the Man with the Red Eyes. In the absence of any ambiguities, or shades of gray, the book's central conflict is clearly and starkly dramatized so that readers of all ages can understand its themes and its message.

Many of the book's central messages are contained in the lessons of life that Meg must learn in order to successfully complete her quest. First, she must learn to overcome her desire for conformity and appreciate her own uniqueness as an individual. In the beginning of the book, Meg feels awkward and out of place at her high school. She is involved in frequent fights with her peers and is sent to the principal's office for her misbehavior. Meg tells her mother that she hates being so different and wishes she could just pretend she is like everyone else. This wish comes terribly true in the form of Camazotz, with its rows of identical houses and identical beings; the planet is a parody of her extreme desire for conformity. Only after she recognizes the evil of this planet does she appreciate the value of being an individual. Outside of this specific plotline, the book also more generally celebrates human creativity and individuality, hailing as heroes the greatest creative geniuses in the arts and sciences, including Einstein, Bach, da Vinci, and Shakespeare.

Another important lesson that Meg must learn is that she cannot know everything. In the beginning of the book, Meg insists that nothing remain unexplained or unquantified. For example, when she meets Calvin, she immediately asks her mother what she thinks of him; she wants an instant and definitive answer. Her mother urges her to be patient, but Meg cannot wait for opinions to form gradually. Meg wants to comprehend everything around her all at once. However, in the course of her travels, she slowly comes to appreciate her mother's words of wisdom: "Just because we don't understand doesn't mean an explanation doesn't exist." She can accept that the musical dance of the creatures on Uriel is beautiful even though she cannot speak their language; she can accept that the Black Thing is evil even though she does not really understand what the Black Thing is. When she ultimately confronts IT on her return visit to Camazotz, she can at last appreciate the dangers of a mind bent on total understanding of definitive and authoritative explanations: such a mind becomes robot-like, mechanical, and unfeeling. Meg's rejection of IT is, thus, also a rejection of the need for total understanding of the world around her.

Yet another theme of the book—and an important lesson for Meg—is the inadequacy of words. Author L'Engle transports her characters to several other planets on which communication takes place through some means other than language. Mrs. Who explains that it is very difficult for her to verbalize her thoughts, and so she usually resorts to quotation.

Aunt Beast tells Meg that "it is not easy at all to put things the way your mind shapes them." The beasts normally communicate nonverbally through their tentacles. Charles Wallace can communicate with Meg by reading her mind. L'Engle, thus, demonstrates that verbal speech is not the only way in which we can share our thoughts and feelings. Meg learns this lesson in her rescue of Charles Wallace: she ultimately triumphs over IT not through eloquent pleas or persuasive rhetoric, but through the sheer power of a love too great for words.

The triumph of love is one of several allusions to Christian theology in the novel. Jesus is the first figure cited by Mrs. Whatsit as a fighter against the Black Thing. Indeed, the whole imagery of light vs. darkness is traced back to the Christian Bible in Mrs. Who's fondness for quotation: "And the light shineth in darkness; and the darkness comprehended it not." In addition, Mrs. Whatsit translates the musical dance of the creatures on Uriel into the biblical words of the prophet Isaiah, and Mrs. Who's second gift to Meg is an excerpt from St. Paul's Epistle to the Corinthians. Yet the characters are never identified as Christians, nor do they engage in any ritualistic religious behavior. Rather, the book refers to Christianity only at the theological or philosophical level; and while the struggle between good and evil forces in the world is a central aspect of Christian theology, it is also universal in its scope. While L'Engle makes explicit references to the Christian Bible, she uses these references merely as a jumping-off point to explore larger, more universal themes.

Summary & Analysis

Chapter 1: Mrs. Whatsit

Summary

On a dark and stormy night, Meg Murry tosses and turns in her attic bedroom. She is unable to fall asleep because she is preoccupied with all that seems wrong in her life: she doesn't fit in at school; her high school teachers have just threatened to drop her down a grade because of her poor academic performance; and worst of all, her father has been missing for many years and no one has heard from him. Meg hears her family's big black dog Fortinbras barking downstairs, and she begins to worry that a stranger may be skulking around the house; she suspects the tramp who, according to local gossip, recently stole twelve bedsheets from the constable's wife, Mrs. Buncombe.

Dismissing her fears as silly and attempting to calm her nerves, Meg decides to make herself some cocoa in the kitchen. She is surprised to find her five-year-old brother Charles Wallace waiting for her at the kitchen table, though she notes that Charles always seems capable of reading her mind. Mrs. Murry soon joins her children and tells Meg that she has received a call from Mrs. Henderson, the mother of the boy Meg had beaten up at school that day. Meg complains to her mother that she hates being an "oddball" at school. She wishes she were more ordinary like her twin younger brothers, Sandy and Dennys. Mrs. Murry tells Meg that she needs to learn the meaning of moderation, the importance of finding a "happy medium." Charles then comments that he has spoken about Meg's problems with his friend Mrs. Whatsit, though he refuses to explain who this woman is.

As Charles Wallace is preparing sandwiches for his mother and sister, Fortinbras begins to bark loudly again. Mrs. Murry goes outside to find the cause of the commotion. She returns with Charles's mysterious friend Mrs. Whatsit, an eccentric tramp completely bundled up in wet clothes. Mrs. Whatsit explains that she glories in nights of such wild weather, but that tonight she has been blown off course in the storm. Charles asks her why she stole bedsheets from Mrs. Buncombe, confirming Meg's suspicion that Mrs. Whatsit is the neighborhood tramp. After removing her boots and drying her feet, Mrs. Whatsit suddenly remarks that "there is such a thing as a tesseract" and then hurries out the door. Mrs. Murry stands very still at the threshold, stunned by Mrs. Whatsit's parting words.

COMMENTARY

This chapter introduces Meg Murry as an ordinary adolescent with many of the same problems facing many teenagers today: she desperately wants to fit in and to feel more comfortable in her identity. She feels like an outcast at school because she doesn't get along with the other students, who accuse her of acting immature. Part of her alienation results from the notoriety of her unusual family: her teachers tell her that they expect her to do better in her classes because both her parents are brilliant scientists; the boys at school make fun of her "dumb baby brother" Charles Wallace, who did not begin to speak until the age of four. Finally, all the townspeople gossip about her absent father, implying that the Murry family should just accept that he has left them. On top of everything else, Meg feels deeply insecure about her personal appearance; compared to her beautiful mother, she describes herself as "repulsive-looking" and wonders whether her social alienation is related to the physical unattractiveness she believes she possesses. Thus, Meg stands out for the very same reasons that make her so representative of most adolescents: awkward and insecure, she lacks confidence in her own abilities.

In contrast to the very typical Meg, Meg's younger brother Charles Wallace is extraordinary—indeed, almost supernatural. Not only does he strike the reader as highly precocious for a five-year-old—preparing liverwurst and cream cheese–sandwiches, conversing freely with old ladies, and teaching himself new vocabulary words—but also Charles Wallace displays an exceptional ability to read the minds of his mother and sister. Mrs. Whatsit, too, exhibits extrasensory powers: she can see the Russian caviar behind a closed cabinet door, and she can somehow sense Meg's distrust of her. These magical abilities introduce the emerging story as one of science fiction and fantasy.

The first chapter not only establishes the tone of the narrative but also foreshadows several important events that will take place over the course of the novel. The description of the moon in the first sentence alludes to the celestial battle between the shadowy Black Thing and the stars witnessed by Meg and her fellow travelers in

Chapter Four: "Every few moments the moon ripped through [the clouds], creating wraithlike shadows that raced across the ground." Meg's mother's remark that Meg needs to learn to find a "happy medium" prefigures Meg's encounter with a creature by this name in Chapter Six. Finally, Mrs. Murry tells Meg that she just needs "to plow through some more time" before things will get easier for her, which is indeed literally what Meg will do when she travels through a wrinkle in time.

CHAPTER 2: MRS. WHO

SUMMARY

Upon awaking the next morning, Meg wonders whether the irrational events of the previous night were merely a dream, but her mother assures her that "you don't have to understand things for them to *be*. That day at school, her social studies teacher sends her to the principal's office for being rude. The principal, Mr. Jenkins, tells Meg that he is sure she could do better in school if only she would apply herself. He asks Meg about her home life, and Meg feels that he is prying when he asks if they have heard from Mr. Murry. She becomes defensive and antagonistic when Mr. Jenkins remarks that the Murrys should just accept that Mr. Murry has left them for good.

After school, Meg, Charles Wallace, and their pet dog Fortinbras go to visit Mrs. Whatsit and her two friends, who have moved into the local haunted house. As they approach the house, Fortinbras begins barking, alerting Meg and Charles Wallace to the presence of Calvin O'Keefe, a popular athlete at Meg's high school. Calvin explains that he is here to escape his family; he is the third of eleven children. But upon further questioning by Charles Wallace, Calvin admits that the haunted house itself also seemed to exert a strong and inexplicable force on him that afternoon. Satisfied by this response, Charles Wallace invites Calvin home with them for dinner.

Before heading back, however, Charles Wallace leads Meg and Calvin into the haunted house. Inside, a plump little woman in large spectacles is busily sewing with Mrs. Buncombe's stolen sheets; a black pot boils on the hearth beside her. Charles refers to this woman as Mrs. Who, and asks her if she knows Calvin. Mrs. Who, who speaks largely in foreign quotations, which she then translates into English, remarks cryptically that Calvin is probably a "good choice." She tells the three children enigmatically that the "time" draws near, but first they must go home and get plenty of food and rest. As they leave the haunted house, Meg begs Charles for an explanation of the woman's strange comments and quotations, but Charles insists that he still doesn't fully understand what is going on. Meg must content herself with this lack of explanation as she, Charles, and Calvin head to the Murry house for dinner.

COMMENTARY

Meg's difficult day at school is a realization of all the fears she had expressed the night before, first while tossing and turning in bed and then while complaining to her mother in the kitchen. She is sent to the principal's office because she has no tolerance for the rote memorization her teacher demands of her. Critics have compared Meg's frustration with the useless information she learns in school to L'Engle's personal frustration with the narrowness of certain Christian doctrines. Just as L'Engle understands her novels as part of a constant quest to find a meaningful theology from among thickets of empty doctrine and repressive dogma, Meg insists on trying to find meaning and purpose in a tedious and seemingly pointless pedagogical exercise.

The two episodes of this chapter, Meg's day at school and her excursion with Charles Wallace, are linked thematically by Meg's inability to comprehend them. At school, she cannot see the point of rote memorization and tedious book learning. After school, she is unable to understand the tacit assumptions and shared sense of purpose that govern the interactions between Charles, Calvin, and Mrs. Who. Her mother's words of wisdom are thus doubly relevant in light of Meg's circumstances: "You don't need to understand things for them to *be*."

Although Charles and Calvin seem to understand more than Meg, they, too, are driven by feelings they do not completely understand. During their walk in the woods, Charles explains to Meg that by concentrating very hard on Meg and Mrs. Murry, he can understand their thoughts. He insists that he does not really understand how this works, because the process seems purely passive: Charles does not feel he must make any effort to "read" his loved ones' minds; rather, he feels that they themselves are freely telling him their thoughts. As Charles tells Meg, "I can't quite explain. You tell me, that's all." Calvin, too, cannot explain the mysterious feeling of compulsion that sometimes overcomes him and demands his obedience: he says, "I can't explain where it comes from or how I get it . . . but I obey it." He does not know why he felt driven to come to the haunted house that afternoon, knowing only that he had no choice in the matter. Thus, all the major characters in the chapter share the sense that they are a part of something that they do not fully understand but that governs their behavior and their interactions with one another.

Already in this second chapter, we see in Meg the power of love that will make possible her ultimate triumph over evil. While walking through the pine forest to the haunted house, Charles Wallace holds her hand and Meg realizes that even if she can know nothing else for certain, she knows her brother loves her; it is this strong sense of love that permits her to rescue her brother from the clutch of IT at the end of the novel.

CHAPTER 3: MRS. WHICH

SUMMARY

Meg, Charles Wallace, and Calvin return to the Murry home, where Mrs. Murry huddles over her Bunsen burner, preparing a dinner of thick stew. Calvin calls his mother to tell her that he will not be home for dinner, though he tells Meg that he doubts his mother would have even noticed his absence. Calvin is deeply moved by the warmth and love that permeates the Murry household, and exclaims to Meg that she is very lucky to have such a wonderful family life.

Before dinner, Meg shows Calvin a picture of her father with a group of scientists at Cape Canaveral. She also helps him with his homework. Calvin is surprised to learn that Meg, who is several grades below him in school, is able to help him with his math and physics. Mrs. Murry explains that Meg's father used to play number games with her when she was a child, teaching her all sorts of tricks and shortcuts.

After dinner, Calvin reads to Charles Wallace in bed while Meg sits with her mother downstairs. Mrs. Murry expresses her grief at her beloved husband's absence. She tells Meg that she believes that things always have an explanation but that these explanations may not always be clear to us. Meg finds this notion troublesome because she likes to think she can understand everything. She comments that Charles Wallace seems to understand more than everyone else, and Mrs. Murry says that this is because Charles is somehow special.

In the evening, Meg and Calvin go out for a walk in the Murrys's backyard. Calvin asks Meg about her father, and she explains that he is a physicist who worked for the government first in New Mexico and then at Cape Canaveral. Meg tells Calvin that the family hasn't heard from their father for a year now, and Calvin alludes to all the rumors that the townspeople circulate about Mr. Murry's whereabouts. Meg becomes immediately defensive, and Calvin is quick to assure her that he has always doubted the rumors' truth. Calvin holds Meg's hand and tells her that her eyes are beautiful; Meg feels herself blushing in the moonlight.

Charles Wallace suddenly appears, announcing that it is time for them to leave on their mission to find Mr. Murry. Mrs. Who slowly materializes in the moonlight and Mrs. Whatsit scrambles over a fence, wearing Mrs. Buncombe's sheets. Then, in a faint gust of wind, their friend Mrs. Which announces in a quivering voice that she, too, is here but will not materialize completely, as the process is too tiring and the little band has much to do.

ANALYSIS

As in the previous chapter, Meg is troubled by all that she does not completely understand. Her first challenge in the novel is to learn to accept not knowing everything. For example, when she first meets Calvin, she immediately wants to form a definitive opinion of him, but her mother urges her to be patient and insists that in time she will come to know him better.

Meg must learn that reality is not always as it seems, a lesson that applies to her father's disappearance, her brother's extraordinary gifts, and her own self-conception. The theme is reinforced at the end of the chapter when Mrs. Which decides to remain invisible, yet her presence is certain. It is Meg's particular challenge to learn to see things more clearly, as they truly are, beneath their often-deceptive surfaces. It is significant that so many of the important characters in the novel wear eyeglasses: Meg points out her father to Calvin as the man in the photo with the glasses; Calvin tells Meg that she has gorgeous eyes behind her glasses; and Mrs. Who's thick spectacles are the first part of her to materialize in the moonlight. The theme of seeing clearly is reinforced later in the novel, when Meg is about to alight on Camazotz with Calvin and her brother; Mrs. Who's parting gift to Meg will be a pair of glasses.

Calvin, too, learns that things are not always as they seem. He is surprised to learn that Meg, although a few grades below him and generally considered a moron at school, is able to help him so much with his homework. Calvin asks Meg several questions about modern physics, all of which she answers readily; ironically, she misses the obvious question about the author of Boswell's *Life of Johnson*. Especially significant is the question about Einstein's equation for the equivalence of mass and energy, for it points to the ideas that influenced L'Engle more generally while she wrote her book. As L'Engle read the latest works of Albert Einstein and Max Planck, she incorporated their ideas about relativity and quantum theory into the conception of time she presents in Chapter Five.

The overarching theme of the book, the power of love, permeates the entire chapter. Calvin remarks that although his mother never seems to notice him, he loves her dearly. Likewise, Mrs. Murry tells Meg that she is "still very much in love" with her husband, even though he has been gone for so long. Calvin is deeply moved by all the love in the Murry household and remarks that the neighbors who invent stories about Mr. Murry's extramarital affairs do so because they "can't understand plain, ordinary love when they see it." Finally, Calvin and Meg's budding romance is also a testament to the power of love even amid adolescent awkwardness: the moonlight glistens on Meg's orthodontic braces and her glasses become stained with tears; yet in Calvin's eyes she appears beautiful.

Chapter 4: The Black Thing

Summary

Meg suddenly feels herself torn apart from Charles and Calvin and thrust into silent darkness. She tries to cry out to them but finds she does not even have a body, much less a voice. Suddenly, she feels her heart beating again and sees Charles and Calvin shimmer back into material presence. Mrs. Whatsit, Mrs. Who, and Mrs. Which inform the children that they are on the planet Uriel. When Calvin inquires into their mode of travel, Mrs. Whatsit explains that they do not travel at any one speed, but rather "tesser" or "wrinkle" through space. Meg wonders if this term relates to the "tesseract" that Mrs. Whatsit mentioned earlier.

Mrs. Whatsit tells the children that the life of their father is threatened, and they are on their way to him, but first they have stopped to learn what they are up against. With Mrs. Who's permission, Mrs. Whatsit transforms herself into a beautiful creature with a horse's body and a human torso. Calvin falls to his knees in shameless devotion, but Mrs. Whatsit admonishes him for his unthinking worship of her.

The children climb on Mrs. Whatsit's back and she flies across fertile fields and a great plateau of granite-like rock. Below, beautiful creatures perform a musical dance in a garden, and Mrs. Whatsit translates their music into the words of the biblical verses of Isaiah 42:10–12. Meg is overcome with joy and instinctively reaches out for Calvin's hand. As they travel upward through the rarefied atmosphere, Mrs. Whatsit hands them each clusters of flowers and tells them to breathe through them when the air becomes too thin.

As they travel through the clouds of Uriel, Mrs. Whatsit shows them a view of the universe not observable from Earth. The children see a great white disk that Mrs. Whatsit identifies as one of Uriel's moons and watch a sunset and moonset. Then, above the clouds, they see a blackness that seems to envelop all the stars around it. Meg knows instinctively that the shadow is the most concentrated form of evil she has ever seen, for it is not cast by any object but is a thing itself. When they return to the flowery fields beneath, Meg walks directly up to Mrs. Which and asks if the Black Thing they saw is what her father is fighting.

ANALYSIS

On the planet Uriel, the children encounter both the tremendous good and the tremendous evil that are currently at battle with each other. The vision of the good, consisting of beautiful creatures engaged in musical dance, compels Meg to hold out her hand to Calvin. Through she does not yet realize it, this love she feels as she reaches out to Calvin will be her ultimate weapon in fighting off the evil forces.

This entire chapter is replete with religious allusions and connotations: the planet Uriel is named for one of the guardian angels of the biblical tradition; and Calvin will eventually compare Mrs. Whatsit, Mrs. Who, and Mrs. Which to guardian angels who travel with and protect them on their cosmic quest. Mrs. Whatsit translates the music of Uriel's beautiful inhabitants into biblical verses; the garden that the travelers fly over resembles Eden in its majesty and serenity, and Meg mentally describes it as "bliss." Finally, Calvin falls to his knees to worship Mrs. Whatsit when she changes her external form, and implicit in her rebuke ("never to me") is the suggestion that there is another Being more worthy of his devotion. These religious motifs reflect L'Engle's passionate commitment to developing her own Christian theology in her writing.

L'Engle's biography also shines through here in the form of the author's use of classical music. L'Engle's mother was a gifted pianist and taught her daughter a fondness for music; L'Engle grew up hearing her mother and other musicians practicing and performing. Many of the characters in her novels are passionate about music, and in this chapter, Mrs. Whatsit speaks in "a rich voice with the warmth of a woodwind, the clarity of a trumpet, the mystery of an English horn." In addition, the biblical verses she quotes are about "singing a new song unto the Lord." This chapter blends L'Engle's Christian orientation and her love of classical music.

CHAPTER 5: THE TESSERACT

SUMMARY

In response to her questioning, Mrs. Which informs Meg that her father is trapped behind the darkness. Mrs. Whatsit assures her that they are traveling to help him. She explains that they travel by tessering, which involves taking shortcuts through time and space. Seeing that Meg remains confused, Charles Wallace explains that tessering is travel in the fifth dimension: the first dimension is a line; the second is a square; the third is a cube; the fourth is Einstein's concept of time; and the fifth is a tesseract. By adding the tesseract to the other four dimensions, they travel in such a way that the shortest distance between two points is not a straight line. Although Meg does not completely understand, she contents herself with this explanation.

A gust of wind blows the children up, and as their bodies dissolve beneath them, Meg and the others find themselves tessering. Suddenly, Meg feels herself stopping; her lungs flatten under a tremendous pressure, and she hears a voice saying that the travelers cannot stop now because they are on a two-dimensional planet. Mrs. Which apologizes to the children for her mistake, noting that she is not used to thinking in a corporeal way; she forgets that human bodies cannot exist in two dimensions.

Mrs. Whatsit explains that they are traveling to a foggy gray planet in the belt of the constellation Orion. Meg expresses concern that her mother will be worried about them back on Earth, but Mrs. Whatsit assures her that they have taken a time wrinkle as well as a space wrinkle; they will arrive back home five minutes before they ever left.

Arriving on the foggy planet, the group enters a cave where Mrs. Whatsit introduces the children to the Happy Medium, a jolly woman in a silk turban and satin gown, bearing a crystal ball.

Mrs. Whatsit asks the Happy Medium to show the children their home planet, but the medium is reluctant to look at something so unpleasant. Meg, Charles, and Calvin see a vision of their planet in which it is surrounded by the Black Thing that they first saw from the atmosphere above Uriel. Mrs. Which explains that the Black Thing is the pure evil that they will have to fight. She assures them that they are not alone; they join a legacy of warriors against the Black Thing, the greatest of which have also been Earthlings: Jesus, da Vinci, Shakespeare, Einstein, Bach, and Gandhi. Impatient, Meg asks about her father; Mrs. Which informs her that he is held captive on a planet that has capitulated to the Black Thing.

ANALYSIS

Whereas the last chapter was most clearly a statement of L'Engle's theology, this chapter presents her understanding of science. She wrote *A Wrinkle in Time* while studying Einstein's theory of relativity, which unites space and time in a single space-time continuum often likened to a fabric. This notion appears in the book when, in demonstrating how the group will travel through space-time, Mrs. Whatsit gathers together the fabric of her skirt.

This chapter also alludes to L'Engle's personal understanding of time, most clearly articulated in her autobiography *A Circle of Quiet*. She explains that there are two types of time: Chronos and Kairos. Whereas Chronos is ordinary clock time, divided evenly into hours, minutes, and seconds, Kairos is God's time, in which notions of past and present are irrelevant. When Meg fears that their mother will worry about her missing children, Mrs. Whatsit assures her that, due to certain properties of time, this will not be the case. The children do not travel through linear time on their journey to rescue Mr. Murry; rather, their quest is circular, involving an escape from ordinary Chronos into the realm of Kairos and then returning to Chronos at a point prior to their departure. L'Engle's creative conception of time resembles the twin paradox and other notions that are a consequence of relativity theory.

Not only does L'Engle further develop the novel's ideas in this chapter, but also she also continues to present us with insights into Meg's character. Again we see Meg's desire to understand everything rationally: when Mrs. Which starts to list the famous fighters of the Black Thing, and the children add to the list from their knowledge of great cultural and historical figures, Calvin and Charles name religious leaders, painters, poets, and musicians, while Meg is able to list only mathematicians and scientists. Her invocation of Euclid and Copernicus reveals Meg's enduring commitment to conquering the world through rational thinking; she has not yet fully accepted the idea of explanations that exceed our logical understanding.

Meg is also reminded of the other lessons she has yet to learn: she must learn to be patient in spite of her desire to rescue her father immediately; she must learn moderation and compromise. Indeed, this latter challenge—first verbalized in Mrs. Murry's advice that Meg seek a "happy medium," and echoed by her twin brothers in Chapter Two—resounds in this chapter as a delightful play on words: Meg and her companions meet a jolly clairvoyant who is, in the most literal sense, a "happy medium." Though this, of course, is not what her mother had in mind, the medium is a playful realization of Mrs. Murry's words and perhaps proves Mrs. Murry wiser than she knows. The encounter also serves to connect Meg back to thoughts of her mother and her mother's advice; although Mrs. Murry cannot be with them, her words' abiding truth lingers with Meg comfortingly.

CHAPTER 6: THE HAPPY MEDIUM

SUMMARY

The Happy Medium next uses her crystal ball to show the children a battle between the Black Thing and the stars. Mrs. Whatsit explains that they have just witnessed a star sacrificing its life to fight the Black Thing, and Charles Wallace correctly guesses that Mrs. Whatsit was once a star who gave up her celestial existence in this way. The children are deeply moved by her sacrifice, and Charles Wallace kisses her as a token of their gratitude.

The Happy Medium wishes to leave the children with a more pleasant vision before they depart, so despite Mrs. Which's protestations, she provides them with a glimpse of their mothers. Calvin's mother, however, is spanking one of her little ones with a wooden spoon, and Meg sees this and reaches out to Calvin compassionately. Mrs. Murry is busy writing her daily letter to her husband, a sight that brings tears to Meg's eyes.

After saying good-bye to the Happy Medium, the group tessers to the planet of Camazotz, where Mr. Murry is imprisoned. They stand on a hill overlooking a town, and Mrs. Whatsit, Mrs. Which, and Mrs. Who inform them that they will not be able to accompany the children into the town. Instead, they supply each child with a gift that will help them in the coming battle. Mrs. Whatsit's "gifts" are really mere enhancements of traits the children already possess: she reinforces in Meg her faults, strengthens Calvin's innate ability to communicate with people of all different types, and bolsters in Charles Wallace the natural resilience of his childhood. Mrs. Who gives Meg her thick funny spectacles, Calvin an excerpt from Shakespeare's *The Tempest*, and Charles a quotation from Goethe. Mrs. Which's "gift" to all three children is the command that they go down into the town and stay strong together. Mrs. Whatsit tells Calvin to take care of Meg and warns Charles that of all the children he will be the most susceptible to the danger on Camazotz. The three children leave their supernatural companions and descend the hill into the town.

In Camazotz, every house is the exact same size, shape, and color. In front of each house, children bounce balls and skip rope in a synchronized rhythm that seems to govern the whole town. One boy drops his ball and when the children knock on the door to return it to the mother, she is horrified by the "Aberration" of a dropped ball. The children are then confronted by a paper delivery boy on a bicycle, who asks them what they are doing out of doors. He informs them that they live in the most oriented city on the planet, governed by IT in the CENTRAL Central Intelligence. When the boy rides off, Charles Wallace notes that he seems to talk as though the words were not his own. Charles concentrates very hard to try to listen to the thoughts of these people, to figure out who they are, but all he hears is a steady pulsing.

Prepared to confront the forces of Camazotz at their source, the children decide to enter the CENTRAL Central Intelligence building. Charles expresses concern that he will not recognize his father after so many years, but Meg reassures him that this will not be a problem. Calvin voices his strong sense that entering the building means facing a terrible danger; however, the children realize that they have no choice.

ANALYSIS

Once again, Meg must accept that reality is not always as it seems. When she learns that Mrs. Whatsit was once a star that gave up its life fighting the Black Thing, she realizes that the creature she knows as Mrs. Whatsit is "only the tiniest facet of all the things Mrs. Whatsit could be." Although Meg does not realize it now, this is also a lesson she will have to apply to her father when he seems powerless to rescue them from Camazotz, to Charles Wallace when he is caught in the grip of IT, and finally to herself when she feels inadequate in the face of IT's tyrannical control. Throughout the course of her travels with Charles and Calvin, Meg learns that people are usually far more complex and capable than they initially appear.

The planet Camazotz represents the dangers of a world devoid of creativity and individuality. Unlike the creative geniuses mentioned in the previous chapter—Einstein, Picasso, Bach, etc.—everyone on Camazotz is exactly like everyone else. The architectural uniformity and total synchrony do not allow for any individuality or freedom of expression. Camazotz, then, is the extreme realization of Meg's desire for conformity: there are no "oddballs" on this planet. Meg must find a happy medium that is neither the extreme conformity represented by Camazotz nor the alienation of her own high school experience, but somewhere between the two.

Camazotz is named for a malignant Mexican deity worshipped as a dark and evil vampire. Critics have suggested that the planet represents Cold War totalitarianism, much like the mechanical, robot-like creatures that inhabit Orwell's *1984*. Other critics interpret Camazotz as a comment on the burgeoning American suburbia, with its rows of identical houses. However, L'Engle never suggests her novel be read historically; rather, she intends her book to portray the timeless struggle between good and evil.

Not only is Camazotz a parody of Meg's personal desire to be like everyone else, but also the evil planet is a parody of her hometown, in that both communities are devoid of love. Faced with an unconventional situation such as Mr. Murry's mysterious disappearance, the gossipy postmistress cruelly assumes the worst, spreading rumors that Mr. Murry has run off with another woman. The postmistress differs little from the mothers on Camazotz who consider the "Aberration" of the dropped ball a cause for horror. In both worlds, there is no room for love amid an overwhelming demand for conformity, order, and logical explanation. Although Meg does not recognize these parallels now, her ultimate understanding of them will enable her to rescue her brother from the clutches of IT.

CHAPTER 7: THE MAN WITH RED EYES

SUMMARY
Calvin wants to enter the CENTRAL Central Intelligence Building by himself and then report back to Meg and Charles Wallace, but the Murry children insist that they heed the parting words of Mrs.

Which and stay together. Just as they are trying to figure out how to enter the building, a door opens before them, revealing a great entrance hall of dull, greenish marble and icy cold walls. Filling the hall are a number of similar-looking men wearing nondescript business suits.

The children decide to ask one of the suited men how things work in CENTRAL. The man instructs them to present their papers to a series of slot machines. He seems unable to understand the fact that they are strangers to the planet and do not know anything about the elaborate mechanical system governing all transactions and interactions. He says that he runs a "number-one spelling machine" on the "second-grade level." He warns that he will have to report the children to the authorities in order to avoid the risk of "reprocessing." Before he leaves, he advises them, "just relax and don't fight it and it will all be much easier for you."

The marble wall in front of the children suddenly dissolves, and they find themselves in an enormous room lined with machines and their robot-like attendants. At the end of the room they approach a platform on which a man with red eyes is seated in a chair. Above his head a glowing light pulsates with the same rhythm as his red eyes. The children immediately sense that the cold blackness emanating from this man is the same as that exuded by the Black Thing, and Charles Wallace instructs Meg and Calvin to close their eyes lest the man hypnotize them. The man tries to do so by having them recite the multiplication tables rhythmically with him, but Charles and Calvin resist by shouting out nursery rhymes and the Gettysburg Address, respectively.

The man speaks directly into the children's brains without opening his mouth or moving his lips. He asks the children why they want to see their father, unable to understand that the sheer fact that he is their father is reason enough. Suddenly, Charles darts forward and kicks the man; he believes that the man is somehow not in full possession of himself. The man tells Charles that of all the children, he is the only one endowed with a neuropsychological system complex enough to understand him; Charles must look into the man's eyes in an attempt to decipher his identity.

The Man with the Red Eyes serves the children an elaborate turkey dinner, but to Charles all the food tastes like sand. The man explains that the food is synthetic, but Charles would be able to taste it if only he would open his mind to IT. He invites Charles to come with him and learn who he really is, and Charles agrees in spite of

Meg's strong protestations. The man stares into Charles Wallace's eyes until the boy's pupils fade into the surrounding blue irises. Once extricated from the man's hypnotic stare, Charles acts like a different person. He asks Meg why she is being so "belligerent and uncooperative" and bids her eat the food prepared for them, which he now claims is delicious. Horrified, Meg shrieks to Calvin that the boy beside them is no longer Charles; the Charles they know is gone.

ANALYSIS

On Camazotz, a reigning uniformity precludes all individuality. However, L'Engle distinguishes between uniformity and togetherness: thus in order to fight the evil forces on the planet, the children must stick together even while maintaining their individual identities. Their togetherness is symbolized by the simple act of holding hands, a gesture that has figured significantly throughout the book: Charles reached for Meg's hand when they walked to the haunted house; Calvin held Meg's hand as they walked through the Murry garden the night after they met Mrs. Who; Meg reached for Calvin's hand when they saw a vision of his mother through the Happy Medium's crystal ball; and now all three children hold hands as they enter the CENTRAL Central Intelligence Building.

The chapter again emphasizes the difference between appearances and reality, for many things on Camazotz are not as they appear. Charles kicks the Man with the Red Eyes because he seems somehow phony; the food that the man serves them appears to be a turkey dinner, but it is really just synthetic food formulated to taste like turkey. To Charles Wallace's penetrating mind, however, the food tastes like sand.

Meg will ultimately realize that the evil force represented by the Man with the Red Eyes lacks one thing that she has—love. Already in this chapter it is apparent that the inhabitants of Camazotz cannot understand love. The Man with the Red Eyes asks Meg why she wants to see her father, not understanding that her filial love for him is reason enough. The exchange recalls Calvin's earlier remark about the gossipy inhabitants of their hometown who invent stories about Mr. Murry's whereabouts; like the Man with the Red Eyes, "They can't understand plain, ordinary love when they see it."

Camazotz further resembles Earth in its inhabitants' expectation of conformity and uniformity. L'Engle writes that the men in the CENTRAL Central Intelligence Building "all wore nondescript business suits, and though their features were as different one from the other as the features of men on earth, there was also a sameness to them." So, too, does life on Earth often include situations in which the only difference among men is their facial features. Nonetheless, as Meg notes, on Camazotz everything adheres to a sameness lacking even at a table of men in corporate dress or a group of tuxedoed gentlemen. Camazotz is uniformity and conformity taken to the extreme.

When Charles calls Meg "belligerent and uncooperative," he echoes the words of her high-school principal Mr. Jenkins, who asked her if she "enjoy[ed] being the most belligerent, uncooperative girl at school." Charles, like Mr. Jenkins, has become a figure of uncompromising and unfeeling authority. His resemblance to Mr. Jenkins underscores the extent to which Meg's journey from Earth by means of a wrinkle in time is also a journey into the psychological content of her own consciousness. Through the transformed Charles Wallace, Meg revisits her memories of a crucial experience on Earth.

CHAPTER 8: THE TRANSPARENT COLUMN

SUMMARY

Charles Wallace, now in the grip of IT, sits contentedly eating his turkey dinner. He tells Meg and Calvin that the Man with the Red Eyes is their friend and that the Mrs. W's are the enemies. They realize that this is not the real Charles Wallace speaking and grab his arm in an attempt to release the real person trapped within. They tell the Man with the Red Eyes that they know that it is he who is speaking through Charles. The Man identifies himself as the Prime Coordinator and tells them that Charles will lead them to Mr. Murry.

Charles leads Meg and Calvin down a long white corridor. As they walk, Meg is reminded of Mrs. Whatsit's gift to Calvin: his ability to communicate. She encourages him to try to speak with her brother. For a moment, Calvin's tone of jocular friendliness seems to reach Charles Wallace, but then the boy drifts away again; Charles tells them that instead of searching for Mr. Murry, they should turn themselves over entirely to IT, whom he identifies as the "Boss" and the "Happiest Sadist." He extols the virtues of IT and declares that on Camazotz, the total conformity prevents all war or unhappiness. Meg notes that sometimes a little bit of unhappiness is a necessary precondition for happiness.

Suddenly, Charles waves his hand and the wall of the corridor grows transparent to reveal a small room radiating a dull, sulphurous light. In response to Meg's questioning, Charles says that he simply moved around the wall's atoms to make it open. He shows Calvin and Meg another room in which the little boy that they saw that afternoon is bouncing a wall to a pulsing rhythm, wincing with pain each time the ball hits the ground; Charles explains that it is a punishment for the boy's earlier deviance. Then he shows Meg and Calvin another small cell, in which stands a transparent cylinder or column; Mr. Murry sits trapped inside.

ANALYSIS

When Charles Wallace advises Meg to "stop fighting and relax," IT is speaking through him. The words echo the counsel of the second grade spelling machine operator who told them, "just relax and don't fight and it will all be much easier for you." Of course, the children know the dangers of submitting; if they fail to fight evil and rescue Mr. Murry, darkness will engulf the world as they know it.

Meg and Calvin try to rescue the real Charles by tightly gripping his arm, an extreme version of the repeated gesture of holding out one's hand in love. Calvin's grip is one of a fierce love only strengthened by the attempts of Camazotz's inhabitants to sever the emotional ties between individuals. Ultimately, however, Calvin's grip is not strong enough to rescue Charles.

Even though Mrs. Whatsit has informed Calvin that his greatest gift is his ability to communicate, Calvin's attempt to win back Charles Wallace through words is just as futile as his effort to reach him by physical touch. Words once again prove woefully inadequate, just as they did when Mrs. Whatsit struggled to translate the beautiful dance on Uriel into speech or when Charles had such difficulty explaining the tesseract in normal language. Charles is only momentarily released from IT when Calvin refers to him affectionately by his silly, playful nickname "Charlibus"; the one "word" that succeeds even partially is a nonsense sound, not a part of a real language at all.

Meg and Calvin's inability to get through to Charles stands in contrast with the ease with which Charles Wallace penetrates walls, enabling the children to walk right through them. Charles explains that he is simply rearranging the configuration of the walls' atoms, since an atom is mostly empty space anyway. Charles' comment bespeaks the influence of quantum theory on L'Engle's scientific views. This theory conceives of the atom as a tiny dense core of protons and neutrons surrounded by great regions of empty space in which tiny electrons appear with varying probabilities. Here, then, Charles claims to rearrange the atoms, merging their regions of empty space into a single material gap in the walls. Although this is not actually possible, the notion gains some credibility in light of quantum physic's atomic model.

Although they are unable to get through to Charles, Meg and Calvin learn about the being that controls him. The newspaper boy mentioned "IT" when he proudly claimed his town's rank as "the most oriented city" on Camazotz; the spelling-machine operator first advised them to submit to IT's control. Now, in this chapter, Charles assures them that they will come to know IT "all in good time." These elliptical references have helped to build the suspense to its current height; Meg and Calvin now stand ready for their encounter with this terrifying being.

CHAPTER 9: IT

SUMMARY

Meg rushes forward to her father in his column, but she cannot penetrate its surface, and her father cannot see or hear her. In frustration, she hurls herself at Charles, but he punches her in the stomach. Calvin nearly releases the real Charles by reciting the lines from Shakespeare's *The Tempest* that Mrs. Who gave him, but Charles ultimately remains in thrall. Finally, at wit's end, Meg remembers Mrs. Who's spectacles. By putting them over her eyes and throwing herself at the column, she successfully gets through to her father and stands by his side.

Mr. Murry is overjoyed at his daughter's arrival, though he cannot see her until he puts on Mrs. Who's spectacles. By wearing the spectacles and carrying Meg in his arms, he is able to escape the column with her. When they emerge, Charles Wallace behaves insolently and obnoxiously toward his father, and Meg assures her father that this is not the real Charles Wallace. Charles tells them that he must take them immediately to IT. Mr. Murry is horrified and insists that Meg will not be able to survive the encounter. However, they have no choice but to follow the youngest Murry child.

Charles leads them out of the CENTRAL Central Intelligence Building and into a strange, domelike edifice pulsing with a violet glow. Inside, Meg feels a steady pulsing that seems to force the beating of her heart to conform to its rhythm. The building contains nothing but the feel of the pulse and a round central dais containing a revoltingly large living brain. Mr. Murry shouts out to Calvin and Meg that they must not give in to IT's rhythmic control. Meg tries to shout out the Declaration of Independence, the periodic table, and the irrational square roots, but her mind nonetheless begins to slip into IT's control.

Seeing that Meg is about to be lost to IT, Calvin commands everyone to tesser. Mr. Murry grabs her wrist and Meg feels herself torn apart in the whirlwind of tessering.

ANALYSIS

In an attempt to fight IT, Meg and Calvin invoke the same creative geniuses who Mrs. Whatsit initially told them had dedicated their lives to waging war with the Black Thing. Thus, Calvin quotes Shakespeare and Meg recites the Declaration of Independence in resistance to the rhythmic of IT's pulsing power. Meg's choice of the Declaration of Independence is significant, for this document protests the principles of conformity and uniformity that characterize a monarchy or, here, life on Camazotz. On Camazotz, people do not have individual rights because they are all exactly the same. Moreover, no one has the freedom of self-determination or the inalienable right to the pursuit of happiness because all of their pursuits are dictated by a cold, disembodied brain.

When the Declaration of Independence fails her, Meg begins reciting the irrational square roots. She cannot recite the rational roots of perfect squares such as 1, 4, and 16, because these will too easily lapse into IT's evil rhythm. Only the irrational roots—with their long, awkward, non-repeating decimal values—stand a chance against IT. Again, this choice is significant; in resisting IT, Meg fights the tyranny of a rational brain devoid of the irrational qualities—the passions, emotions, and foibles—that make us human.

By representing IT with a disembodied brain, L'Engle comments on the dangers of intellect untempered by emotion. Such pure rationality precludes individuality; without emotion, people are mechanical, robot-like creatures identical to one another. Only when we can feel love and pain can we think creatively and develop as unique individuals.

Attempting to fight IT on the strength of his exceptional intelligence, Charles Wallace fails to withstand the evil force; his intellect alone is not sufficient. Charles's downfall results from his failure to heed the advice of the Mrs. W's: Mrs. Whatsit told him to beware of pride and arrogance, but Charles still thought that he could resist

IT single-handedly; Mrs. Who warned him to remember that he does not know everything, but Charles warmed to the Man with the Red Eyes when he praised his neuropsychological complexity; Mrs. Which told all of the children to stay together at all times, but Charles insisted on going off with the Man in the CENTRAL Central Intelligence Building. Charles's downfall demonstrates that intelligence and intellect alone cannot resist the tyranny of uniformity.

CHAPTER 10: ABSOLUTE ZERO

SUMMARY

As Meg regains consciousness, she feels icy coldness all around her and finds herself unable to move her body or speak. She hears the voices of Calvin and her father discussing her condition, but she has no way of communicating with them.

Meg hears Calvin ask her father about his journey to Camazotz. Mr. Murry explains that he never intended to go to this planet; he was part of a team of scientists trying to tesser to Mars. Mr. Murry says that he knows he could not have been on Camazotz for longer than two years, but time seems to flow differently on this planet. He tells Calvin that he was about to give up all hope and surrender to IT when the children arrived to rescue him.

Meg desperately tries to make a sound to let her father and Calvin know that she can hear them. She finally succeeds in making a small croaking noise, slowly regaining the ability to speak. She demands to know where Charles Wallace is, and she is furious to learn that they left Camazotz without him. She yells at her father for his inability to solve their difficulties and deliver them all to safety. Mr. Murry tells his daughter that he is only a fallible human being, and no miracle worker; however, he expresses the belief that "all things work together for good for them that love God."

Mr. Murry massages Meg's fingers, and she cries out in pain. He tells her that the pain is a good sign; it means she is regaining sensation. Suddenly, Calvin tells them to look ahead of them. Three strange upright creatures advance toward them, each with four arms; they have tentacles in place of hair, and soft indentations where their eyes would be were they human. Calvin introduces himself politely to the creatures, and explains Meg's precarious condition. At first Meg is terrified, but when one of the creatures reaches out to touch her with its wavy tentacle, warmth spreads through her body. The creature picks her up and tells Mr. Murry that it is taking Meg with it.

ANALYSIS

The title of this chapter, "Absolute Zero," is a scientific term for the temperature at which all molecular motion ceases, –273 degrees Celsius. Meg experiences this dangerously low temperature when she tessers with her father through the Black Thing. Thus, when she wakes up, she is so cold that she cannot feel her own body.

Meg's faint pulse is barely detectable to Mr. Murry and Calvin, in striking contrast to the overwhelmingly dominant and unavoidable pulse of IT's rhythmic brain. When Meg awakens, it is as if she has been in a coma; she struggles to recover her senses. Her struggle to communicate with her father recalls Calvin's struggle to communicate with the possessed Charles Wallace and Meg's own attempt to get through to her father when he was imprisoned in the glass column.

When Meg winces in pain as her father massages her fingers, he tells her that the pain is actually good, for it means that she is able to feel again. Meg learned the emotional equivalent of this physical lesson while still on Camazotz: on this planet the inhabitants are never unhappy, but this is because they are unable to feel any emotions at all; pain and sorrow are a natural and necessary part of the ability to feel.

In this chapter, L'Engle demonstrates that evil is not merely external, as Meg would like to believe. Meg unfairly blames her father for failing to rescue Charles Wallace; although she fails to realize it, her self-righteous accusation is characterized by the same evil exuded by IT and the Black Thing. As L'Engle writes, "she did not realize that she was as much in the power of the Black Thing as Charles Wallace." Meg will only later understand that she is often threatened by internal evils just like the one possessing Charles Wallace externally.

Meg lashes out at her father because she cannot accept that he is merely a fallible human being like herself. She expects him to be superhuman and to solve all their problems. Like all children, Meg is going through the difficult experience of realizing that her parents do not know everything. Only when she abandons this naive view of her father will she fully mature and be able to value her own unique abilities and potential. Ultimately, it is not Mr. Murry, but Meg herself, who will save Charles Wallace.

CHAPTER 11: AUNT BEAST

SUMMARY

In answer to the tentacled creatures' questions, Calvin explains that he is a young man from a planet engaged in fighting off the Black Thing. The beasts seem surprised that Calvin and the Murrys are not used to meeting beings from other planets. They tell their guests that they must entrust Meg to their care because she is extremely vulnerable and weak.

Meg leans against the soft, furry chest of one of the beasts and feels warm and secure. The beasts rub something warm over her body, clothe her in fur, and serve her something "completely and indescribably delicious." She begins talking with one of the beasts, who encourages Meg to think of an appropriate name for her. After dismissing *mother*, *father*, *acquaintance*, and *monster*, Meg settles on the epithet, *Aunt Beast*. Meg tries to explain light and vision to Aunt Beast, who has no eyes. At the creature's urging, Meg falls into a deep sleep and wakes up feeling wonderfully rested.

Aunt Beast tells Meg that it finds communication in Meg's language very difficult, Still, it tries to explain that the beasts live on a planet called Ixchel, another of the planets struggling against the Black Thing. It then sings to Meg a beautiful song that sets Meg at peace with herself and the world.

After clothing and comforting Meg once more, Aunt Beast takes her back to her father and Calvin, who are eating a delicious but colorless meal prepared by the beasts. Meg asks impatiently whether they have tried to summon the three Mrs. W's. Meg tries to describe these women to Aunt Beast but realizes that all physical description is useless when speaking with a creature that cannot see. She concentrates very intently on the essence of these three extraordinary women, then suddenly hears Mrs. Which's thundering voice announcing their arrival.

ANALYSIS

The planet Ixchel is named for the Mayan goddess of the rainbow and patron of medicine. This name is appropriate because Ixchel, like the biblical rainbow of the Noah's ark story, offers Meg the opportunity for renewal and restoration, even though the planet is devoid of color. In addition, the creatures act as medics, nursing Meg back to health after her dangerous brush with the Black Thing.

In this chapter, L'Engle challenges our fundamental assumptions about how people communicate with one another and perceive the world. Mrs. Whatsit had told Calvin that his gift was his ability to communicate with all types of creatures, and Calvin's gift at last proves useful as he struggles to explain their situation in a language that the creatures can understand. The creatures are not used to ordinary speech; their words are vocalized through their tentacles in an entirely different language. Aunt Beast tells Meg that her language is "so utterly simple and limited that it has the effect of extreme complication." Most of the wonderful things on Ixchel cannot be described in words: Aunt Beast's singing is "impossible to describe . . . to a human being"; it feeds Meg "something completely and indescribably delicious" and it tells Meg that it has great difficulty expressing things the way her mind shapes them. Aunt Beast's discomfort with human language is evident from its grammatical and syntactic irregularities, such as "Would you like me to take you to your father and your Calvin?"

The creatures demonstrate the ability to read Meg's thoughts. For example, Aunt Beast's mind can join Meg's as Meg thinks of possible names for it. This type of extrasensory perception resembles Charles's ability to know Meg's thoughts, as well as the ability of the Man with the Red Eyes to bore into the children's minds. In separating verbal speech from communication, L'Engle shows that language is only one possible way of relating to one another.

Similarly, by separating sight from perception, L'Engle demonstrates that seeing is only one way of coming to know and understand the world. When challenged to explain the concepts of "light" and "sight" to Aunt Beast, Meg realizes the extent to which her sense of the world is informed by vision. This lesson is reemphasized later in the chapter when she must describe the Mrs. W's without referring to their physical appearance.

The disassociation between sight and perception functions to reinforce one of the novel's major themes: the relationship between appearances and reality. Aunt Beast tells Meg, "Think about things as they *are*. This *look* doesn't help us at all." The difference between form and essence is also relevant to the type of food that the beasts serve Calvin and the Murrys. Unlike the food on Camazotz, which looked delicious but tasted like sand to Charles Wallace, the food on Ixchel is gray and dull but tastes wonderfully delicious. In creating a planet where perceiving does not mean seeing and communicating does not mean speaking in words, L'Engle keenly reinforces the primary themes of her novel.

CHAPTER 12: THE FOOLISH AND THE WEAK

SUMMARY

Mrs. Whatsit, Mrs. Who, and Mrs. Which materialize on Ixchel in response to Meg's summons. However, they insist that they can do nothing to help save Charles Wallace. Mr. Murry requests that they help him with his tessering so he can try to retrieve Charles from Camazotz, but Mrs. Which tells him he will not be successful. Next, Calvin asks to be sent after Charles, but he, too, is refused. After a long silence, Meg realizes that everyone expects her to go back to Camazotz and rescue her brother. Terrified and overwhelmed by the weight of this responsibility, Meg yells that she cannot go back. She gradually realizes, however, that she is the one who is closest with Charles and the one who is most likely to get through to him, to bring him back successfully. Although her father and Calvin do not want to let her go, the Mrs. W's ultimately convince them that it is for the best.

Meg says good-bye to her father, Calvin, and Aunt Beast and also apologizes to her father for her accusatory outbursts. Mrs. Which tells Meg that she will tesser with her through the Black Thing so that Meg will arrive at Camazotz safely. Once again each of the Mrs. W's presents Meg with a gift: Mrs. Whatsit enhances the force of her innate love; Mrs. Who gives her a blessing from the Christian Bible; and Mrs. Which strengthens in her the one thing that she has that IT has not. However, Meg must discover this thing for herself.

After tessering with Mrs. Which, Meg arrives safely on Camazotz and heads directly to the domelike building where IT lies waiting. Inside, Charles Wallace crouches behind the dais containing the disembodied brain; his eyes roll and a tic in his forehead pulses to IT's revolting rhythm. Meg tries to identify Mrs. Which's gift, while Charles insists that she has nothing that IT does not also have; her weapon cannot be her ability to resist, her anger, or her hatred, for IT has all of these things.

Charles tells Meg that Mrs. Whatsit hates her, and at that moment, Meg realizes the one thing that she has that IT does not have: love. Though she cannot possibly love IT, she *can* love Charles Wallace, and she calls out to him with the force of her love. Suddenly, he runs into her arms and the children tesser together through the darkness. When they emerge from the darkness, they find they have rejoined Calvin and Mr. Murry in the twins' vegetable garden back on Earth!

After a joyous family reunion, the three Mrs. W's appear. Mrs. Whatsit apologizes for not saying good-bye; the Mrs. W's are busy with a new mission. She starts to describe the mission, but at that moment, there is a gust of wind and before Mrs. Whatsit can complete her sentence, the three extraordinary ladies are gone.

ANALYSIS

All of the gifts that Meg receives in this chapter allude to Christian theology. Mrs. Whatsit and Mrs. Which strengthen Meg with both their love and her own love, and Mrs. Which gives her an excerpt from St. Paul's Epistle to the Corinthians. This biblical passage offers empowerment to the foolish and the weak and charges human beings to fulfill their calling despite their sense of inadequacy.

Left to discover Mrs. Which's gift for herself, Meg gains the power of free choice. Throughout the novel, characters make small but important decisions that affect the entire universe: these include Charles Wallace's decision to visit Mrs. Whatsit, the children's decision to make the journey, and Meg's return trip to Camazotz. In empowering her characters with freedom of choice, L'Engle rejects notions of determinism. She believes that life is like a sonnet—organized and structured but not predetermined. As Mrs. Whatsit tells Calvin, "You're given the form, but you have to write the sonnet yourself. What you say is completely up to you." When Meg decides to return to Camazotz, she writes another line in the sonnet of her life.

Meg returns to Earth a changed person, even though no chronological time has elapsed. Finally confident in who she is, she understands that she does not need to conform in order to make positive contributions to the world. Meg discovers that the power of selfless love can set her free just as it released Charles Wallace from the clutches of IT. Thus, her cosmic quest to prevent the Black Thing's conquest of the universe is also a deeply personal quest: having successfully completed it, Meg is able to accept herself and her own abilities; she is ready to make her own contribution to the world.

STUDY QUESTIONS

1. *What are the most important lessons that Meg learns over the course of the novel?*

Meg must learn 1) the value of individuality and 2) to accept that not everything can be understood rationally. First, she must learn to overcome her desire for conformity and appreciate her own uniqueness as an individual. In the beginning of the book, Meg feels awkward and out of place at her high school. She is involved in frequent fights with her peers and is sent to the principal's office for her misbehavior. Meg tells her mother that she hates being an oddball and wishes she could just pretend she was like everyone else. Camazotz, then, with its rows of identical houses and identical beings, parodies her extreme desire for conformity. Only after she understands the evil of this planet does she realize the value of being a unique individual. The book celebrates human creativity and individuality, hailing as heroes the greatest creative geniuses in the arts and sciences including Einstein, Bach, da Vinci, and Shakespeare. Another important lesson that Meg must learn is that she cannot know everything. In the beginning of the book, Meg insists that nothing remain unexplained or unquantified. For example, when she meets Calvin, she immediately asks her mother what she thinks of him; she wants an instant and definitive answer. Her mother urges her to be patient, but Meg cannot wait for opinions to form gradually. Meg wants to comprehend everything around her all at once. However, in the course of her travels, she slowly comes to appreciate her mother's words of wisdom: "Just because we don't understand doesn't mean an explanation doesn't exist." She can accept that the musical dance of the creatures on Uriel is beautiful even though she cannot speak their language; she can accept that the Black Thing is evil even though she does not really understand what it is. When she ultimately confronts IT on her return visit to Camazotz, she can at last appreciate the dangers of a mind bent on total understanding, on definitive and authoritative explanations: such a mind becomes robot-like, mechanical, and unfeeling. Meg's rejection of IT is also a rejection of the need for total understanding of the world around her.

2.   *In what ways can* A Wrinkle in Time *be considered a*
      Christian book? Is this a fair characterization?

A Wrinkle in Time can be considered a Christian book in the sense that its most important theme is the centrality of love, a notion equally important to Christian theology. Ultimately, Meg is only able to conquer IT through the force of her love for her brother. The novel also contains many explicit references to Christian scripture. Jesus is the first figure cited by Mrs. Whatsit as a fighter against the Black Thing, and the whole imagery of light vs. darkness is traced back to the Christian Bible by Mrs. Who in her fondness for quotation: "And the light shineth in darkness; and the darkness comprehended it not." In addition, Mrs. Whatsit translates the musical dance of the creatures on Uriel into the biblical words of the prophet Isaiah, and Mrs. Who's second gift to Meg is an excerpt from St. Paul's Epistle to the Corinthians. Yet the characters are never identified as Christians, neither do they engage in any ritualistic religious behavior. Rather, the book is informed by Christian theology and by the notion of a struggle between good and evil forces in the world. In spite of its explicit references to the Christian Bible, the themes that L'Engle treats are essential components of any religious worldview.

3.   *How are women portrayed in L'Engle's novel?*

The women in L'Engle's novel are strong, competent, self-reliant, and intelligent individuals. Mrs. Murry is an experimental biologist who has mastered the skill of balancing family and career: she conducts groundbreaking scientific research while nurturing a warm and loving family, even if this means an occasional dinner cooked on a Bunsen burner. The three Mrs. W's travel competently through the fifth dimension—a skill they have mastered far better than Meg's father. Finally, although Meg initially feels awkward and insecure, she, too, emerges as a self-confident and triumphant heroine; ultimately, it is Meg alone (without the aid of her father, brother, or Calvin) who rescues Charles Wallace from IT. By writing a science fiction novel with a female protagonist, L'Engle paved the way for many other female protagonists in a genre traditionally dominated by male heroes. Her cast of intellectually talented women was unusual in the 1960s, though today the competent female protagonist is far more common.

How to Write Literary Analysis

The Literary Essay: A Step-by-Step Guide

When you read for pleasure, your only goal is enjoyment. You might find yourself reading to get caught up in an exciting story, to learn about an interesting time or place, or just to pass time. Maybe you're looking for inspiration, guidance, or a reflection of your own life. There are as many different, valid ways of reading a book as there are books in the world.

When you read a work of literature in an English class, however, you're being asked to read in a special way: you're being asked to perform *literary analysis*. To analyze something means to break it down into smaller parts and then examine how those parts work, both individually and together. Literary analysis involves examining all the parts of a novel, play, short story, or poem—elements such as character, setting, tone, and imagery—and thinking about how the author uses those elements to create certain effects.

A literary essay isn't a book review: you're not being asked whether or not you liked a book or whether you'd recommend it to another reader. A literary essay also isn't like the kind of book report you wrote when you were younger, where your teacher wanted you to summarize the book's action. A high school- or college-level literary essay asks, "How does this piece of literature actually work?" "How does it do what it does?" and, "Why might the author have made the choices he or she did?"

The Seven Steps

No one is born knowing how to analyze literature; it's a skill you learn and a process you can master. As you gain more practice with this kind of thinking and writing, you'll be able to craft a method that works best for you. But until then, here are seven basic steps to writing a well-constructed literary essay:

1. Ask questions
2. Collect evidence
3. Construct a thesis

4. Develop and organize arguments
5. Write the introduction
6. Write the body paragraphs
7. Write the conclusion

---

1. ASK QUESTIONS

When you're assigned a literary essay in class, your teacher will often provide you with a list of writing prompts. Lucky you! Now all you have to do is choose one. Do yourself a favor and pick a topic that interests you. You'll have a much better (not to mention easier) time if you start off with something you enjoy thinking about. If you are asked to come up with a topic by yourself, though, you might start to feel a little panicked. Maybe you have too many ideas—or none at all. Don't worry. Take a deep breath and start by asking yourself these questions:

- **What struck you?** Did a particular image, line, or scene linger in your mind for a long time? If it fascinated you, chances are you can draw on it to write a fascinating essay.

- **What confused you?** Maybe you were surprised to see a character act in a certain way, or maybe you didn't understand why the book ended the way it did. Confusing moments in a work of literature are like a loose thread in a sweater: if you pull on it, you can unravel the entire thing. Ask yourself why the author chose to write about that character or scene the way he or she did and you might tap into some important insights about the work as a whole.

- **Did you notice any patterns?** Is there a phrase that the main character uses constantly or an image that repeats throughout the book? If you can figure out how that pattern weaves through the work and what the significance of that pattern is, you've almost got your entire essay mapped out.

- **Did you notice any contradictions or ironies?** Great works of literature are complex; great literary essays recognize and explain those complexities. Maybe the title (*Happy Days*) totally disagrees with the book's subject matter (hungry orphans dying in the woods). Maybe the main character acts one way around his family and a completely different way around his friends and associates. If you can find a way to explain a work's contradictory elements, you've got the seeds of a great essay.

At this point, you don't need to know exactly what you're going to say about your topic; you just need a place to begin your exploration. You can help direct your reading and brainstorming by formulating your topic as a *question,* which you'll then try to answer in your essay. The best questions invite critical debates and discussions, not just a rehashing of the summary. Remember, you're looking for something you can *prove or argue* based on evidence you find in the text. Finally, remember to keep the scope of your question in mind: is this a topic you can adequately address within the word or page limit you've been given? Conversely, is this a topic big enough to fill the required length?

GOOD QUESTIONS

"Are Romeo and Juliet's parents responsible for the deaths of their children?"

"Why do pigs keep showing up in LORD OF THE FLIES*?"*

"Are Dr. Frankenstein and his monster alike? How?"

BAD QUESTIONS

"What happens to Scout in TO KILL A MOCKINGBIRD*?"*

"What do the other characters in JULIUS CAESAR *think about Caesar?"*

"How does Hester Prynne in THE SCARLET LETTER *remind me of my sister?"*

---

2. COLLECT EVIDENCE

Once you know what question you want to answer, it's time to scour the book for things that will help you answer the question. Don't worry if you don't know what you want to say yet—right now you're just collecting ideas and material and letting it all percolate. Keep track of passages, symbols, images, or scenes that deal with your topic. Eventually, you'll start making connections between these examples and your thesis will emerge.

Here's a brief summary of the various parts that compose each and every work of literature. These are the elements that you will analyze in your essay and which you will offer as evidence to support your arguments. For more on the parts of literary works, see the Glossary of Literary Terms at the end of this section.

ELEMENTS OF STORY   These are the *what*s of the work—what happens, where it happens, and to whom it happens.

- **Plot:** All of the events and actions of the work.

- **Character:** The people who act and are acted upon in a literary work. The main character of a work is known as the *protagonist.*

- **Conflict:** The central tension in the work. In most cases, the protagonist wants something, while opposing forces (antagonists) hinder the protagonist's progress.

- **Setting:** When and where the work takes place. Elements of setting include location, time period, time of day, weather, social atmosphere, and economic conditions.

- **Narrator:** The person telling the story. The narrator may straightforwardly report what happens, convey the subjective opinions and perceptions of one or more characters, or provide commentary and opinion in his or her own voice.

- **Themes:** The main idea or message of the work—usually an abstract idea about people, society, or life in general. A work may have many themes, which may be in tension with one another.

ELEMENTS OF STYLE   These are the *how*s—how the characters speak, how the story is constructed, and how language is used throughout the work.

- **Structure and organization:** How the parts of the work are assembled. Some novels are narrated in a linear, chronological fashion, while others skip around in time. Some plays follow a traditional three- or five-act structure, while others are a series of loosely connected scenes. Some authors deliberately leave gaps in their works, leaving readers to puzzle out the missing information. A work's structure and organization can tell you a lot about the kind of message it wants to convey.

- **Point of view:** The perspective from which a story is told. In *first-person point of view,* the narrator involves him or herself in the story. ("I went to the store"; "We watched in horror as the bird slammed into the window.") A first-person narrator is usually the protagonist of the work but not always. In *third-person point of view,* the narrator does not participate in the story. A third-person narrator may closely follow a specific character, recounting that individual character's thoughts or experiences, or it may be what we call an *omniscient* narrator. Omniscient narrators see and know all: they can witness any event in any time or place and are privy to the inner thoughts and feelings of all characters. Remember that the narrator and the author are not the same thing!

- **Diction:** Word choice. Whether a character uses dry, clinical language or flowery prose with lots of exclamation points can tell you a lot about his or her attitude and personality.

- **Syntax:** Word order and sentence construction. Syntax is a crucial part of establishing an author's narrative voice. Ernest Hemingway, for example, is known for writing in very short, straightforward sentences, while James Joyce characteristically wrote in long, incredibly complicated lines.

- **Tone:** The mood or feeling of the text. Diction and syntax often contribute to the tone of a work. A novel written in short, clipped sentences that use small, simple words might feel brusque, cold, or matter-of-fact.

- **Imagery:** Language that appeals to the senses, representing things that can be seen, smelled, heard, tasted, or touched.

- **Figurative language:** Language that is not meant to be interpreted literally. The most common types of figurative language are *metaphors* and *similes,* which compare two unlike things in order to suggest a similarity between them— for example, "All the world's a stage," or "The moon is like a ball of green cheese." (Metaphors say one thing *is* another thing; similes claim that one thing is *like* another thing.)

LITERARY ANALYSIS

---

3. CONSTRUCT A THESIS

When you've examined all the evidence you've collected and know how you want to answer the question, it's time to write your thesis statement. A *thesis* is a claim about a work of literature that needs to be supported by evidence and arguments. The thesis statement is the heart of the literary essay, and the bulk of your paper will be spent trying to prove this claim. A good thesis will be:

- **Arguable.** "*The Great Gatsby* describes New York society in the 1920s" isn't a thesis—it's a fact.

- **Provable through textual evidence.** "*Hamlet* is a confusing but ultimately very well-written play" is a weak thesis because it offers the writer's personal opinion about the book. Yes, it's arguable, but it's not a claim that can be proved or supported with examples taken from the play itself.

- **Surprising.** "Both George and Lenny change a great deal in *Of Mice and Men*" is a weak thesis because it's obvious. A really strong thesis will argue for a reading of the text that is not immediately apparent.

- **Specific.** "Dr. Frankenstein's monster tells us a lot about the human condition" is *almost* a really great thesis statement, but it's still too vague. What does the writer mean by "a lot"? *How* does the monster tell us so much about the human condition?

Good Thesis Statements

Question: In *Romeo and Juliet*, which is more powerful in shaping the lovers' story: fate or foolishness?

Thesis: "Though Shakespeare defines Romeo and Juliet as 'star-crossed lovers' and images of stars and planets appear throughout the play, a closer examination of that celestial imagery reveals that the stars are merely witnesses to the characters' foolish activities and not the causes themselves."

Question: How does the bell jar function as a symbol in Sylvia Plath's *The Bell Jar*?

Thesis: "A bell jar is a bell-shaped glass that has three basic uses: to hold a specimen for observation, to contain gases, and to maintain a vacuum. The bell jar appears in each of these capacities in *The Bell Jar,* Plath's semi-autobiographical novel, and each appearance marks a different stage in Esther's mental breakdown."

Question: Would Piggy in *The Lord of the Flies* make a good island leader if he were given the chance?

Thesis: "Though the intelligent, rational, and innovative Piggy has the mental characteristics of a good leader, he ultimately lacks the social skills necessary to be an effective one. Golding emphasizes this point by giving Piggy a foil in the charismatic Jack, whose magnetic personality allows him to capture and wield power effectively, if not always wisely."

4. Develop and Organize Arguments

The reasons and examples that support your thesis will form the middle paragraphs of your essay. Since you can't really write your thesis statement until you know how you'll structure your argument, you'll probably end up working on steps 3 and 4 at the same time.

There's no single method of argumentation that will work in every context. One essay prompt might ask you to compare and contrast two characters, while another asks you to trace an image through a given work of literature. These questions require different kinds of answers and therefore different kinds of arguments. Below, we'll discuss three common kinds of essay prompts and some strategies for constructing a solid, well-argued case.

Types of Literary Essays

- **Compare and contrast**

    Compare and contrast the characters of Huck and Jim in THE ADVENTURES OF HUCKLEBERRY FINN.

    Chances are you've written this kind of essay before. In an academic literary context, you'll organize your arguments the same way you would in any other class. You can either go *subject by subject* or *point by point*. In the former, you'll discuss one character first and then the second. In the latter, you'll choose several traits (attitude toward life, social status, images and metaphors associated with the character) and devote a paragraph to each. You may want to use a mix of these two approaches—for example, you may want to spend a paragraph apiece broadly sketching Huck's and Jim's personalities before transitioning into a paragraph or two that describes a few key points of comparison. This can be a highly effective strategy if you want to make a counterintuitive argument—that, despite seeming to be totally different, the two characters or objects being compared are actually similar in a very important way (or vice versa). Remember that your essay should reveal something fresh or unexpected about the text, so think beyond the obvious parallels and differences.

- **Trace**

    Choose an image—for example, birds, knives, or eyes—and trace that image throughout MACBETH.

    Sounds pretty easy, right? All you need to do is read the play, underline every appearance of a knife in *Macbeth*, and then list them in your essay in the order they appear, right? Well, not exactly. Your teacher doesn't want a simple catalog of examples. He or she wants to see you make *connections* between those examples—that's the difference between summarizing and analyzing. In the *Macbeth* example, think about the different contexts in which knives appear in the play and to what effect. In *Macbeth,* there are real knives and imagined knives; knives that kill and knives that simply threaten. Categorize and classify your examples to give them some order. Finally, always keep the overall effect in mind. After you choose and analyze your examples, you should come to some greater understanding about the work, as well as your chosen image, symbol, or phrase's role in developing the major themes and stylistic strategies of that work.

- **Debate**

  Is the society depicted in 1984 good for its citizens?

  In this kind of essay, you're being asked to debate a moral, ethical, or aesthetic issue regarding the work. You might be asked to judge a character or group of characters (*Is Caesar responsible for his own demise?*) or the work itself (*Is* JANE EYRE *a feminist novel?*). For this kind of essay, there are two important points to keep in mind. First, don't simply base your arguments on your personal feelings and reactions. Every literary essay expects you to read and analyze the work, so search for evidence in the text. What do characters in *1984* have to say about the government of Oceania? What images does Orwell use that might give you a hint about his attitude toward the government? As in any debate, you also need to make sure that you define all the necessary terms before you begin to argue your case. What does it mean to be a "good" society? What makes a novel "feminist"? You should define your terms right up front, in the first paragraph after your introduction.

  Second, remember that strong literary essays make contrary and surprising arguments. Try to think outside the box. In the *1984* example above, it seems like the obvious answer would be no, the totalitarian society depicted in Orwell's novel is *not* good for its citizens. But can you think of any arguments for the opposite side? Even if your final assertion is that the novel depicts a cruel, repressive, and therefore harmful society, acknowledging and responding to the counterargument will strengthen your overall case.

5. WRITE THE INTRODUCTION

Your introduction sets up the entire essay. It's where you present your topic and articulate the particular issues and questions you'll be addressing. It's also where you, as the writer, introduce yourself to your readers. A persuasive literary essay immediately establishes its writer as a knowledgeable, authoritative figure.

An introduction can vary in length depending on the overall length of the essay, but in a traditional five-paragraph essay it should be no longer than one paragraph. However long it is, your introduction needs to:

- **Provide any necessary context.** Your introduction should situate the reader and let him or her know what to expect. What book are you discussing? Which characters? What topic will you be addressing?

- **Answer the "So what?" question.** Why is this topic important, and why is your particular position on the topic noteworthy? Ideally, your introduction should pique the reader's interest by suggesting how your argument is surprising or otherwise counterintuitive. Literary essays make unexpected connections and reveal less-than-obvious truths.

- **Present your thesis.** This usually happens at or very near the end of your introduction.

- **Indicate the shape of the essay to come.** Your reader should finish reading your introduction with a good sense of the scope of your essay as well as the path you'll take toward proving your thesis. You don't need to spell out every step, but you do need to suggest the organizational pattern you'll be using.

Your introduction should not:

- **Be vague.** Beware of the two killer words in literary analysis: *interesting* and *important*. Of course the work, question, or example is interesting and important—that's why you're writing about it!

- **Open with any grandiose assertions.** Many student readers think that beginning their essays with a flamboyant statement such as, "Since the dawn of time, writers have been fascinated with the topic of free will," makes them sound important and commanding. You know what? It actually sounds pretty amateurish.

LITERARY ANALYSIS

- **Wildly praise the work.** Another typical mistake student writers make is extolling the work or author. Your teacher doesn't need to be told that "Shakespeare is perhaps the greatest writer in the English language." You can mention a work's reputation in passing—by referring to *The Adventures of Huckleberry Finn* as "Mark Twain's enduring classic," for example—but don't make a point of bringing it up unless that reputation is key to your argument.

- **Go off-topic.** Keep your introduction streamlined and to the point. Don't feel the need to throw in all kinds of bells and whistles in order to impress your reader—just get to the point as quickly as you can, without skimping on any of the required steps.

----

6. WRITE THE BODY PARAGRAPHS

Once you've written your introduction, you'll take the arguments you developed in step 4 and turn them into your body paragraphs. The organization of this middle section of your essay will largely be determined by the argumentative strategy you use, but no matter how you arrange your thoughts, your body paragraphs need to do the following:

- **Begin with a strong topic sentence.** Topic sentences are like signs on a highway: they tell the reader where they are and where they're going. A good topic sentence not only alerts readers to what issue will be discussed in the following paragraph but also gives them a sense of what argument will be made *about* that issue. "Rumor and gossip play an important role in *The Crucible*" isn't a strong topic sentence because it doesn't tell us very much. "The community's constant gossiping creates an environment that allows false accusations to flourish" is a much stronger topic sentence— it not only tells us *what* the paragraph will discuss (gossip) but *how* the paragraph will discuss the topic (by showing how gossip creates a set of conditions that leads to the play's climactic action).

- **Fully and completely develop a single thought.** Don't skip around in your paragraph or try to stuff in too much material. Body paragraphs are like bricks: each individual one needs to be strong and sturdy or the entire structure will collapse. Make sure you have really proven your point before moving on to the next one.

- **Use transitions effectively.** Good literary essay writers know that each paragraph must be clearly and strongly linked to the material around it. Think of each paragraph as a response to the one that precedes it. Use transition words and phrases such as *however, similarly, on the contrary, therefore,* and *furthermore* to indicate what kind of response you're making.

---

7. WRITE THE CONCLUSION

Just as you used the introduction to ground your readers in the topic before providing your thesis, you'll use the conclusion to quickly summarize the specifics learned thus far and then hint at the broader implications of your topic. A good conclusion will:

- **Do more than simply restate the thesis.** If your thesis argued that *The Catcher in the Rye* can be read as a Christian allegory, don't simply end your essay by saying, "And that is why *The Catcher in the Rye* can be read as a Christian allegory." If you've constructed your arguments well, this kind of statement will just be redundant.

- **Synthesize the arguments, not summarize them.** Similarly, don't repeat the details of your body paragraphs in your conclusion. The reader has already read your essay, and chances are it's not so long that they've forgotten all your points by now.

- **Revisit the "So what?" question.** In your introduction, you made a case for why your topic and position are important. You should close your essay with the same sort of gesture. What do your readers know now that they didn't know before? How will that knowledge help them better appreciate or understand the work overall?

- **Move from the specific to the general.** Your essay has most likely treated a very specific element of the work—a single character, a small set of images, or a particular passage. In your conclusion, try to show how this narrow discussion has wider implications for the work overall. If your essay on *To Kill a Mockingbird* focused on the character of Boo Radley, for example, you might want to include a bit in your conclusion about how he fits into the novel's larger message about childhood, innocence, or family life.

- **Stay relevant.** Your conclusion should suggest new directions of thought, but it shouldn't be treated as an opportunity to pad your essay with all the extra, interesting ideas you came up with during your brainstorming sessions but couldn't fit into the essay proper. Don't attempt to stuff in unrelated queries or too many abstract thoughts.

- **Avoid making overblown closing statements.** A conclusion should open up your highly specific, focused discussion, but it should do so without drawing a sweeping lesson about life or human nature. Making such observations may be part of the point of reading, but it's almost always a mistake in essays, where these observations tend to sound overly dramatic or simply silly.

A+ Essay Checklist

Congratulations! If you've followed all the steps we've outlined, you should have a solid literary essay to show for all your efforts. What if you've got your sights set on an A+? To write the kind of superlative essay that will be rewarded with a perfect grade, keep the following rubric in mind. These are the qualities that teachers expect to see in a truly A+ essay. How does yours stack up?

- ✓ Demonstrates a thorough understanding of the book
- ✓ Presents an original, compelling argument
- ✓ Thoughtfully analyzes the text's formal elements
- ✓ Uses appropriate and insightful examples
- ✓ Structures ideas in a logical and progressive order
- ✓ Demonstrates a mastery of sentence construction, transitions, grammar, spelling, and word choice

Suggested Essay Topics

1. *In what ways does Camazotz resemble Meg's neighborhood on Earth?*

2. *In what way is* A Wrinkle in Time *informed by Madeleine L'Engle's personal theological and scientific ideas?*

3. *How are Mrs. Whatsit, Mrs. Who, and Mrs. Which distinguished from one another?*

4. *Why does L'Engle represent IT as a large disembodied brain? What is the symbolism of this?*

5. *Describe what makes Charles Wallace so extraordinary. How do these traits both hurt and help him on Camazotz?*

6. *What are the various non-linguistic ways in which the creatures in this book communicate with one another? Do you think that L'Engle believes that words are ultimately inadequate as a method of communication?*

7. *What is the significance of the lack of sight among the beast-like inhabitants of Ixchel? What does Meg learn from interacting with creatures that have no eyes?*

GLOSSARY OF LITERARY TERMS

ANTAGONIST

The entity that acts to frustrate the goals of the *protagonist*. The antagonist is usually another *character* but may also be a non-human force.

ANTIHERO / ANTIHEROINE

A *protagonist* who is not admirable or who challenges notions of what should be considered admirable.

CHARACTER

A person, animal, or any other thing with a personality that appears in a *narrative*.

CLIMAX

The moment of greatest intensity in a text or the major turning point in the *plot*.

CONFLICT

The central struggle that moves the *plot* forward. The conflict can be the *protagonist*'s struggle against fate, nature, society, or another person.

FIRST-PERSON POINT OF VIEW

A literary style in which the *narrator* tells the story from his or her own *point of view* and refers to himself or herself as "I." The narrator may be an active participant in the story or just an observer.

HERO / HEROINE

The principal *character* in a literary work or *narrative*.

IMAGERY

Language that brings to mind sense-impressions, representing things that can be seen, smelled, heard, tasted, or touched.

MOTIF

A recurring idea, structure, contrast, or device that develops or informs the major *themes* of a work of literature.

NARRATIVE

A story.

NARRATOR

The person (sometimes a *character*) who tells a story; the *voice* assumed by the writer. The narrator and the author of the work of literature are not the same person.

PLOT

The arrangement of the events in a story, including the sequence in which they are told, the relative emphasis they are given, and the causal connections between events.

POINT OF VIEW

The *perspective* that a *narrative* takes toward the events it describes.

PROTAGONIST

The main *character* around whom the story revolves.

SETTING

The location of a *narrative* in time and space. Setting creates mood or atmosphere.

SUBPLOT

A secondary *plot* that is of less importance to the overall story but that may serve as a point of contrast or comparison to the main plot.

SYMBOL

An object, *character,* figure, or color that is used to represent an abstract idea or concept. Unlike an *emblem,* a symbol may have different meanings in different contexts.

SYNTAX

The way the words in a piece of writing are put together to form lines, phrases, or clauses; the basic structure of a piece of writing.

THEME

A fundamental and universal idea explored in a literary work.

TONE

The author's attitude toward the subject or *characters* of a story or poem or toward the reader.

VOICE

An author's individual way of using language to reflect his or her own personality and attitudes. An author communicates voice through *tone, diction,* and *syntax.*

LITERARY ANALYSIS

A Note on Plagiarism

Plagiarism—presenting someone else's work as your own—rears its ugly head in many forms. Many students know that copying text without citing it is unacceptable. But some don't realize that even if you're not quoting directly, but instead are paraphrasing or summarizing, it is plagiarism unless you cite the source.

Here are the most common forms of plagiarism:

- Using an author's phrases, sentences, or paragraphs without citing the source
- Paraphrasing an author's ideas without citing the source
- Passing off another student's work as your own

How do you steer clear of plagiarism? You should always acknowledge all words and ideas that aren't your own by using quotation marks around verbatim text or citations like footnotes and endnotes to note another writer's ideas. For more information on how to give credit when credit is due, ask your teacher for guidance or visit www.sparknotes.com.

LITERARY ANALYSIS

Review & Resources

Quiz

1. In what is Mr. Murry imprisoned?

    A. A tesseract
    B. A transparent column
    C. A discmbodied brain
    D. A crystal ball

2. Which of the following is NOT one of Meg's greatest faults?

    A. Impatience
    B. Anger
    C. A need to understand everything
    D. Suspicion of her brother's unusual powers

3. Where does the final scene of the book take place?

    A. In the garden outside the Murrys' house
    B. In Mrs. Murry's laboratory
    C. In Mr. Jenkins's office
    D. On Uriel

4. What do the creatures on Ixchel use to communicate?

    A. Their soft facial indentations
    B. Their numerous tentacles
    C. Their layers of soft fur
    D. Their flapping wings

5. Calvin O'Keefe is popular in school as a(n)

    A. Scholar
    B. Musician
    C. Artist
    D. Athlete

6.   Which of the following characters never leaves Earth?

    A.   Mrs. Buncombe
    B.   Mrs. Whatsit
    C.   Aunt Beast
    D.   Mr. Murry

7.   Which of the following is NOT true of Mrs. Murry?

    A.   She writes letters to her husband every night
    B.   She sometimes cooks dinner for her family on her
        Bunsen burner
    C.   She is a physicist working on a top-secret government
        project
    D.   She believes that her son Charles Wallace is special

8.   Where was Mr. Murry trying to tesser to when he
inadvertently landed on Camazotz?

    A.   Earth
    B.   Mars
    C.   Ixchel
    D.   Uriel

9.   All of the following characters are associated with goodness
and light EXCEPT:

    A.   The Happy Medium
    B.   Aunt Beast
    C.   The Man with the Red Eyes
    D.   Mrs. Which

10.   Which of the following characters transforms herself into a
beautiful centaur?

    A.   Mrs. Whatsit
    B.   Mrs. Who
    C.   Aunt Beast
    D.   Mrs. Jenkins

11. Which is NOT true of this novel?

    A. It won the Newbery Prize
    B. It has been translated into more than fifteen languages
    C. It is part of a series of books about time
    D. It was written exclusively for children and young adults

12. Which of the following is not found on Camazotz?

    A. The CENTRAL Central Intelligence Building
    B. The twins' vegetable garden
    C. The transparent column
    D. The paper delivery boy

13. All of the following characters usually wear glasses EXCEPT:

    A. Meg
    B. Mr. Murry
    C. Mrs. Who
    D. Calvin O'Keefe

14. What kind of food does The Man with the Red Eyes serve to the children?

    A. Turkey
    B. Liverwurst and cream cheese sandwiches
    C. Russian caviar
    D. A thick homemade stew

15. Which of the following characters is most vulnerable to the danger of tessering through the Black Thing?

    A. Charles Wallace
    B. Meg
    C. Mr. Murry
    D. Calvin O'Keefe

REVIEW & RESOURCES

16.   Who is the oldest of the following characters?

   A.   Mrs. Whatsit
   B.   Mrs. Which
   C.   Mrs. Who
   D.   Mrs. Buncombe

17.   Mrs. Whatsit compares life to a

   A.   Sonnet
   B.   Painting
   C.   Musical score
   D.   Ball game

18.   A *Wrinkle in Time* is classified as belonging to all of the following genres EXCEPT:

   A.   Horror
   B.   Science fiction
   C.   Fantasy
   D.   Young-adult fiction

19.   Meg receives all of the following gifts EXCEPT:

   A.   Mrs. Whatsit's love
   B.   Mrs. Who's spectacles
   C.   An excerpt from the Christian Bible
   D.   A stolen bedsheet

20.   L'Engle's theory of time was influenced by all of the following EXCEPT:

   A.   Albert Einstein's relativity theory
   B.   Max Planck's quantum theory
   C.   The Greek concept of *kairos*
   D.   Nostradamus's predictions

21.   The children see all of the following through the Happy Medium's crystal ball EXCEPT:

   A.   Mrs. Murry
   B.   Mrs. O'Keefe
   C.   The Earth engulfed by a dark shadow
   D.   The rhythmic pulse of IT

22. What is Meg's strongest subject at school?

   A.   Chemistry
   B.   Math
   C.   History
   D.   English

23. Meg's father has worked at all of the following places and institutions EXCEPT:

   A.   The Smithsonian Institute for Astrophysics at Harvard
   B.   The Institute for Higher Learning in Princeton
   C.   New Mexico
   D.   Cape Canaveral, Florida

24. At different points in the novel, the various characters describe Mrs. Whatsit as all of the following EXCEPT:

   A.   A tramp
   B.   A witch
   C.   A shadow
   D.   A star

25. Which of the following is NOT a reason why Charles Wallace is considered an unusual child?

   A.   He did not begin speaking until very late
   B.   He has an exceptionally large vocabulary
   C.   He taught himself to read before he entered school
   D.   He can read his sister's mind

26. Which of the following is NOT used as a weapon against IT?

   A.   The Declaration of Independence
   B.   Love
   C.   The periodic table
   D.   Nuclear power

27. Who is Fortinbras?

   A.   Mrs. Whatsit's imaginary friend
   B.   The Murrys' pet dog
   C.   A character in Shakespeare's *The Tempest*
   D.   A jolly clairvoyant

SUGGESTIONS FOR FURTHER READING

Hettinga, Donald R. *Presenting Madeleine L'Engle.* New York: Twayne Publishers, 1993. L'Engle, Madeleine.*A Circle of Quiet.* San Francisco: Harper, 1972.

L'Engle, Madeleine. *A Wrinkle in Time.* New York: Dell Publishing, 1962.

Marecki, Joan E. "Madeleine L'Engle." In *Contemporary Authors (New Revision Series),* Vol. 21. Detroit: Gale Research Inc., 1987.

Parker, Marygail G. "Madeleine L'Engle." In *Dictionary of Literary Biography,* Vol. 52. Detroit: Gale Research Inc., 1986.

REVIEW & RESOURCES